On the Road with Mallory

For Adam, the best son
a mother could ask for
—L.B.F.

For my husband, Josh, who keeps me
laughing through it all
—J.K.

by Laurie Friedman
illustrations by Jennifer Kalis

MINNEAPOLIS

CONTENTS

A WORD FROM MALLORY

My name is Mallory McDonald, like the restaurant. Even though we're not related, we have more in common than just a name: McDonald's is always busy and so am I.

At least I have been this summer. From the moment fourth grade ended, I haven't stopped.

First, Chloe Jennifer left for the summer to go stay with her Grandma. Then Mary Ann and Joey moved to a new house on the other side of Fern Falls. With no friends left on Wish Pond Road, I thought for sure I was going to have the most boring summer ever.

But, I've been helping Mrs. Black in her garden. I took an art class. And Grandma came to visit

This way

and taught me how to bake a peanut butter pie and a chocolate fudge cake.

This summer has turned out to be really fun, and it's about to get even more fun.

In five days, my family is going on a road trip to the Grand Canyon, and I can't wait! Even Max says he's excited too. My parents have planned tons of fun activities.

We're visiting a petrified forest, going white-water rafting, and taking a mule ride down into the Grand Canyon. Mom has been making snacks for the past week, and Dad took me to the mall to buy Mad Libs to do on the way there, plus a new journal so I can write about all the fun stuff we do on our trip.

I've been waiting all summer for this vacation to get here and now that it almost is, I'm so, so, so excited! NOTHING can get in the way of the most amazing trip ever!

ABSOLUTELY NOTHING!

Mallory McDonald's
Trip Journal
I ♥
ROAD
TRIPS

Grand Canyon,
Here We Come!
Speed Limit 65
Read On
STOP
ONE WAY

Oh great!
Cousin Kate!!
Fashion Fran
Don't open!

A Change of Plans

THREE DAYS TO GO . . .
AND COUNTING!

Dear Trip Journal,

We're not leaving on our trip for three days but I already have something to write about in my journal, and it's NOT GOOD! Mom, Dad, Max, and I aren't the only people who will be together on this trip.

My cousin Kate is coming too!

I was SHOCKED when I found out! Even though Kate's mom and my dad are brother and sister, we don't see that side of our family very often. Aunt Julie, Uncle Mark, and Kate live far away in Chicago, and my aunt and uncle are both busy doctors.

And when we do see them, it doesn't go well. Last year, they visited us for a few days over winter break, and each day that they were here, Dad said less and less to Aunt Julie. I think the problem was that Aunt Julie said a lot of things that annoyed Dad.

It's kind of like how Max says things that annoy me, and (according to Max) I say lots of things that annoy him (even though I don't think I do that very often).

I asked Dad about it after they left, and he said he and Aunt Julie just don't have a lot in common. I get that, because Kate and I don't have much in common either. Even though we're almost the same age, we're COMPLETELY different.

Here are just a few examples of how we're different:

Example #1: I like to watch TV and Kate doesn't.

The last time she and her parents were here, I was watching Fashion Fran and I said to Kate, "You really should watch Fashion Fran because it is probably the best TV show ever made." Then I told her that Mary Ann and I have never missed an episode.

She shook her head like that was something she would NEVER do and said, "Mallory, watching TV makes your brain shrink."

Then she said, "Mallory, given how much Fashion Fran you've watched, your brain is probably very small for a girl your age."

It's not that I eat junk food all the time. But Kate says she doesn't eat it AT ALL.

One day during that same visit when Kate told me watching TV makes your brain shrink, I ate a doughnut in front of her, and Kate made a face like I was making a HUGE mistake. Then she said, "Mallory, DON'T eat that! Doughnuts are full of trans fat."

I wasn't even sure what trans fat was, but by the look on her face, I figured it wasn't good. I knew if I asked what she meant she would give me a long lecture on why I shouldn't be eating the doughnut.

So I did the only thing I could do: I pretended like I didn't hear what she'd said (even though she'd said it pretty loudly), and kept eating my doughnut.

Example #3: I have a brother and a dog and Kate doesn't.

She always says she's SOOOOO glad she doesn't have any of those things.

When she's around, if Max and I start fighting (which is unfortunately quite often), she says things like, "I'm SOOOOO

glad I don't have to waste my time arguing with someone I live with."

And when she sees me doing something for Cheeseburger, like cleaning out her litter box, or if she sees Max feeding Champ, she wrinkles her nose and holds her stomach and says, "I'm SOOOOO lucky I don't have a pet that I have to take care of."

It's not like I mind that Kate and I are different. It just means we don't have a lot to talk about when we're together.

And we're about to be together for a LONG TIME!

Tonight at dinner, Mom and Dad told us that Kate is going to fly to meet us in Fern Falls, and then she'll be with us for our entire vacation.

"WHY?" asked Max, like he couldn't think of one reason that Mom and Dad could think it would be a good idea for her to come with us.

But Dad had an explanation. "Uncle Mark and Aunt Julie are busy with work, and they want Kate to be able to do something fun with family this summer."

Max shook his head like he thought this was a lame reason. But he didn't say anything else—at least not until later.

After dinner, Max and I sat on his bed and talked about it.

"I don't like how Kate acts as if she's so much smarter than we are—and how she's always trying to teach us stuff," I said.

Max nodded. "Yeah," he said. "That's really annoying. But the worst part is that whenever she's around, we always end up getting into trouble."

Max reminded me about how he tried to show Kate how to play basketball the last time she was here. "Remember how she kept reading the history of basketball to me and I told her to stop reading and start playing? She got mad and told Aunt Julie I pushed her. I got in trouble even though I was trying to be nice."

I nodded. "And remember how Kate told me we should secretly open my Christmas presents? Then, after she helped me tape them all back up and said no one would ever know, she told mom that she saw me in her closet secretly opening them all by myself!"

"How could I forget that?" said Max. "You got into so much trouble."

Even though Max and I don't always agree on things, we do agree that having Kate coming along on the trip is probably not the best idea.

But hopefully, we're both wrong.

Mallory

GRAND
CANYON
THIS WAY→
Time is of
the Essence!

Ready. Set.

ONE DAY TO GO

Dear Trip Journal,

We're not leaving until tomorrow, but we have a lot to do today. At least according to mom.

She says max and I have to finish packing this morning because Kate will get here this afternoon, and she doesn't want us packing when we should be spending time with our cousin.

When mom said that, max rolled his eyes and shot me a look. I could tell spending time with Kate wasn't exactly at the top of his to-do list. To be honest, it wasn't exactly at the top of mine either.

Even though max was the one who did the eye rolling, mom gave both of us

a speech about being nice to Kate, and how this trip should be a "good growth experience" for her.

Then she looked at her watch and said time was of the essence (an expression I learned in school which means you don't have a minute to waste, which isn't even the case because we have a whole morning to pack and only one small suitcase each to pack in.)

Mom just said, "Go pack. Now!"

G.2.G. (Got to go.) G.2.P. (Got to pack.)

♥ Mallory

IN MY ROOM PACKING

Dear Trip Journal,

The answer to the question above is NO! All my stuff can NOT fit in my suitcase.

For the last hour, I've been trying to fit the clothes I need for this vacation into the suitcase mom gave me. I tried folding my clothes and shoving my clothes. I even had max sit on my suitcase so I could zip it shut.

But no matter what I did, my suitcase would not close.

So I went to get mom and told her I need a bigger suitcase. I thought it was a pretty smart solution, but it didn't work. mom told me we have limited luggage space so I need to, "narrow down my wardrobe choices."

G.2.G. (Got to go.) G.2.N. (Got to narrow.)

Then I have to drive to the airport with my family to pick up Kate.

Mallory

HOME FROM THE AIRPORT

Dear Trip Journal,

We just got home from the airport and you won't believe what happened!

Once we got Kate, we went to baggage claim to get her suitcase which was **HUGE!!!**

I couldn't believe how big it was!

Right when I saw it, I said to Kate, "We have limited luggage space. You're going to have to narrow down your wardrobe choices."

I thought for sure mom was going to say, "That's right, Kate. Mallory already narrowed down her choices. Now it's your turn."

But all mom said was, "Kate's suitcase is fine."

You probably can't believe that's what I just wrote. Join the club. I couldn't believe it was what I heard!

☹ Mallory

BEFORE DINNER

Dear Trip Journal,

I don't mean to complain, but since the whole point of having you is to write what I'm feeling, I'm going to be honest and write that I'm not all that happy that Kate is coming on this trip with us.

Ever since we got home from the airport, I've been trying to be happy about it, but Kate hasn't made it easy.

I asked Kate if she wanted to paint her toenails. "We can paint them the same color so they match on the trip."

I thought it was a really good idea. Mary Ann and I love to have matching toenails.

But Kate didn't think it was such a good idea. "Toenail painting is a waste of time," she said.

I wanted to say that toenail painting is not a waste of time, but I knew she would have lots of reasons for why she thinks it is. I also knew mom would get mad if she thought I was arguing with Kate already, so I let it go.

Since Kate didn't want to paint her toenails, I thought she might like going to the wish pond. But when I suggested it, she said she didn't want to do that either.

"Mallory, you know there's no such thing as a wish pond. It's just a pond."

When Kate said that, I really didn't want to do anything with her, so I sat down on my bed and started reading.

I guess Kate thought that was a good idea, because she sat down beside me and we stayed like that for the rest of the afternoon.

This way

But to be perfectly honest, I didn't enjoy it.

Mallory

AFTER DINNER

Dear Trip Journal,

Before dinner, I thought I might not be happy about Kate coming on this trip with us. Now I KNOW I'm not happy about it. She just said so many things at dinner that made it so hard to think that spending the next two weeks together will be fun.

When Dad said, "How was your school year?"

Kate said, "I didn't get any B's."

"Wow! You made all A's?" Dad said, even though that seemed pretty obvious.

"Actually, I made all A+'s," said Kate.

Max rolled his eyes. Mom saw him, but even she could tell Kate was being annoying so she tried changing the subject. "Kate, are you still riding horses?" she asked.

This way

Kate smiled. I thought maybe it was going to be a good topic to discuss with her, but I was wrong.

"I won so many medals and awards competing this year that Mom and Dad are turning our guest room into a trophy room."

Max shook his head like he couldn't believe he had to listen to this conversation. Then he started texting under the table with his new cell phone.

"Max, please put that away," said Mom. She gave him a be-polite-to-our-guest look.

Since I don't have a cell phone, I just tried to concentrate on my food instead of on Kate's bragging.

The rest of the dinner went pretty much the same way. When Mom brought out the special night-before-our-trip strawberry shortcake she made for dessert, she started telling Kate about all the fun things we have planned for the trip.

When she was done, she looked at Kate. It was pretty obvious that it was Kate's turn to say something like, "Wow! That sounds like so much fun!"

But what Kate said was, "I've already been to London, Paris, and Hong Kong."

When I was helping Mom clear the table, I said (quietly and in the kitchen so Kate couldn't hear), "Since Kate has already been to London, Paris, and Hong

This way

Kong, maybe she doesn't want to go to the Grand Canyon. It might be boring for her."

But all Mom said back was, "Mallory, please stack the dishes in the sink." I think that was code for "Like it or not, Kate is coming with us to the Grand Canyon."

At 6 a.m. tomorrow morning, the journey begins.

Mallory

BORING!
Just the Facts!
JOURNAL
History & FUN FACTS
Mad Libs
MOO.....
Shhhh!!! Shhhh!
SECRETS!
Shhhhh!

Off We Go!

DAY 1

Dear Trip Journal,

It's not easy to write in a journal while you're driving in a van, but there's not much else to do. It's only 9 a.m and I've already eaten breakfast (and a snack), drawn two pictures, read ten pages of my summer reading book, and done a mad Lib with Kate (who wasn't that much fun to do it with because I misspelled some of the words she used.)

When Kate saw the finished Mad Lib, she announced out loud that I'd misspelled three words, and mom asked to see them. Then she gave me a lecture about the importance of good spelling.

I put away the Mad Libs, but when I did, things went from bad to worse.

Kate got out her tablet and said, "As we travel, I'll be sharing lots of history and fun facts with you about the places we'll be visiting."

First she told us several fun facts about the Grand Canyon, which were actually kind of cool to know.

Then she started reading the history of the Grand Canyon. Since it has been around for millions of years, it apparently has a lot of history, and I'm pretty sure Kate read all of it to us.

Kate's GRAND CANYON FUN FACTS:

#1: The Grand Canyon is millions of years old.

#2: It is 277 miles long, up to 18 miles across and 1 mile deep.

#3: The Grand Canyon is one of the seven wonders of the world.

Even though I liked hearing about the Grand Canyon, Kate had been reading for a very long time, and it was starting to get on my nerves.

I could tell it was annoying Max too, because he put his head against the window like he was trying to go to sleep. Then he put his sweatshirt over his head.

I was trying to think of a nice way to ask Kate to stop reading. The good news is that Max beat me to it. The bad news is that he didn't do it in a nice way.

He pointed to her tablet and said, "If you don't put that thing away, I'm going to throw it out the window."

"MAX!" Both my parents said his name in a you-know-you're-not-allowed-to-talk-like-that tone.

"Sorry!" said Max. "But it's impossible to sleep while she's reading."

When he said that, Kate put her tablet in her bag and said to Max, "Sorry if you don't like knowing things about the places you visit. I like learning as much as I can."

Max just rolled his eyes and started texting on his phone.

Then Kate added, "I guess that makes me a smart traveler."

Even though she was acting like what Max said hadn't bothered her, I could tell she was a little hurt.

I think Mom and Dad could tell too.

"That does make you smart," said Dad.

"Yes," said Mom. "But I think we all might benefit from doing our own things for a few minutes. I knew that was her way of saying no one should talk to anyone else until we had something to say the other person would like hearing.

But unfortunately, someone didn't like hearing what Kate said next.

"Who are you texting?" Kate asked Max.

When Max didn't answer, Kate asked him again.

"Why do you want to know?" asked Max.

I kind of don't blame him for saying that. It wasn't any of Kate's business.

But Mom turned around and said, "Max, be nice to your cousin."

"Kate doesn't need to know who I'm texting," he said in a really annoyed voice.

I have to admit I don't know why he was acting like it was a big secret. The only people Max ever texts are the guys

on his baseball team and his girlfriend, Winnie.

"I don't want to have to ask you again to be nice," said Mom. We're all on this vacation together, and everyone needs to make a special effort to get along.

"I can do that," said Kate. Then she looked at Max. "Can he?"

"Yeah," grumbled Max. But I think he only said it because Mom was looking at him like she was waiting for an answer.

"Let's all play the Quiet Game," said Dad. Then he smiled into the rearview mirror like he thought his idea was a good one and expected each one of us to play.

So that's what I've been doing. Sitting here quietly, staring out the window at mile after mile of road. The most interesting things I've seen are cows.

And most of them have been sleeping.

This car ride is taking forever!!!!!!!!!!!!!!!!!!

☹ Mallory

Oklahoma City

Oklahoma!

WE'RE HERE!
STOP #1

Dear Trip Journal,

We've arrived! We're not at our final destination, the Grand Canyon. But we just got to the hotel in Oklahoma City. I'm very happy to be here, mainly because it means I'm no longer in the car, which I was in for a veeeeeeeeery looooooong tiiiiiiiiiime!

G.2.G. (Got to go.) G.2.S.M.L. (Got to stretch my legs.) Then I have to find the pool which Mom and Dad said Kate and Max and I could go to for a before-dinner swim.

♥☺♥ *Mallory*

SHORTEST SWIM EVER

Dear Trip Journal,

Swimming wasn't as much fun as I thought it would be because we didn't get to swim for long. Right when we got to the pool, Kate asked me if I had a boyfriend.

I said no. Then, Kate asked Max if he had a girlfriend.

"Why do you need to know?" asked Max.

I don't think Max asked the question in a very friendly way, and based on

Kate's response, I don't think she thought so either.

"I was just trying to be nice," Kate said. Then she made a face like Max had hurt her feelings.

I sent Max a just-tell-her-what-she-wants-to-know look.

"I have a girlfriend," he said.

"What's her name?" asked Kate.

"Winnie," Max said grumpily. Then he dove under the water.

"Hmmm. Interesting," said Kate, sounding like she wasn't done exploring this topic.

I knew Max wasn't going to like it if Kate kept asking him questions about

Winnie, so I decided to jump in. "Winnie is Joey's big sister and Mary Ann's stepsister," I explained. I'd already told Kate about my friends and how they'd also been our neighbors until they moved across town at the beginning of the summer, so I knew she would get the connection.

Then Max came up for air, and I tried to send Kate an it's-time-to-change-the-subject look. Unfortunately, it didn't work.

Kate looked at Max and said, "I'm surprised your girlfriend's name is Winnie. I thought it might be . . ."

But before Kate could say anything else, Max cut her off. "I'm sick of talking about this!" he snapped at her.

That's when Kate got out of the pool and wrapped a towel around herself.

"You're not being very nice," she said. Then she walked back into the hotel.

"Do you think she's going to tell on me?" asked Max.

I could tell by the look on his face that he thought that's exactly what she was going to do, and so did I. We both grabbed our towels and followed her into the elevator.

"Sorry," Max mumbled to Kate when the doors closed.

The good news is that Kate said she accepted Max's apology, but the bad news is that when Max suggested we forget about it and go back to the pool, Kate said it would be hard to forget about it and that she was going to the room with or without us.

So that's why our swim was so short.

☹ Mallory

P.S. Kate was being pretty annoying about the whole what's-your-girlfriend's-name thing, But Max was Kind of overly sensitive about it, which makes me wonder . . . WHY????

A DAY OF PROBLEMS

Dear Trip Journal,

When I woke up this morning, I hoped the day would be problem free. But it was problem FILLED. The problems started this morning at the first place we visited, the Oklahoma History Center.

It's this huge museum all about the history of Oklahoma. A lot of interesting things have happened in Oklahoma over the years, and as you walk through the

This way

Oklahoma History Center, you can read all about them. As we walked through the exhibits, Mom, Dad, Max, and I were all reading to ourselves about different events.

The problem was that Kate was reading everything out loud.

Mom and Dad actually both asked Kate to try and read a little more quietly. I think they asked her because other people looked like they were getting annoyed listening to Kate read.

Then Max said, "This is supposed to be a self-guided tour, which means you DON'T need to read to others."

I thought that did the trick because Kate stopped reading out loud, but she also stopped talking and didn't say a word to anyone until we left the museum.

When we were in the car on the way to our next activity, which was supposed to be to a place called Frontier City (a major theme park and major fun!) and then to an outlet mall (also major fun!), Kate got out her tablet. "We are very close to one of the biggest botanical gardens in the country," she said. "It would be a shame not to stop there."

So we did.

Mom and Dad both agreed it was worth a stop. So when we should have

This way

been riding roller coasters and buying cute clothes, we were looking at flowers, plants, and trees.

That wouldn't have been a problem, except that there were 17,000 acres of flowers, plants, and trees to look at, so it took a really long time, which meant that when we left, we didn't have time to go to BOTH Frontier City AND the outlet mall today.

"You kids can choose which place we go," said Mom.

"I want to go to Frontier City," said Max.

"I want to go to the outlet mall," I said.

"Since no one can agree, why don't we go to the Banjo Museum?" said Kate.

"We're going to have to draw straws," said Dad. "That's the only fair way. So we drew straws. And guess where we went?!?

If you guessed the Banjo Museum, you guessed right.

Even though I really wanted to go to the outlet mall or Frontier City, I learned two cool things at the Banjo Museum (and not because Kate told me either one of them).

Cool thing #1: The Banjo Museum has over 300 types of banjos. I was surprised to learn that there were that many types. Seeing all of them was pretty interesting

Cool thing #2: The museum also has a gift shop that sells postcards. They had a lot of kinds (but not 300) that showed different pictures of Oklahoma. I bought one to mail to Mary Ann and one to put in here as a memory of my trip to Oklahoma City.

When we got back to the room after dinner, Kate got out her tablet and read us a bunch of stuff about the state of Oklahoma.

As Kate kept reading, I was having a hard time focusing on what she was saying because I kept thinking about the fact that Grandma's nickname for me and Oklahoma's state insect are one and the same.

Kate's Oklahoma FUN FACTS:

#1: The state bird is the scissor-tailed flycatcher.

#2: The state insect is the honeybee.

#3: Oklahoma's state nickname is the Sooner state.

It was also hard because while she was reading about Sooners (which was a nickname for early Oklahoma settlers), Max was mumbling that he'd like it if she'd stop reading sooner vs. later so he could focus on what he was doing, which was texting.

Kate finally stopped, but I think that was only because Dad came into our room and said it was lights out and early to bed for everyone. We're back on the road tomorrow. Goodbye, Oklahoma. New Mexico, here we come!

Mallory

Oklahoma City

One Big joy Ride. NOT!

Oh no!

Yikes!!

Albuquerque

On the Road Again

ON OUR WAY TO NEW MEXICO MORE PROBLEMS

Dear Trip Journal,

I don't mean for the theme of this journal to be "PROBLEMS." But, we seem to be having lots of them on this trip.

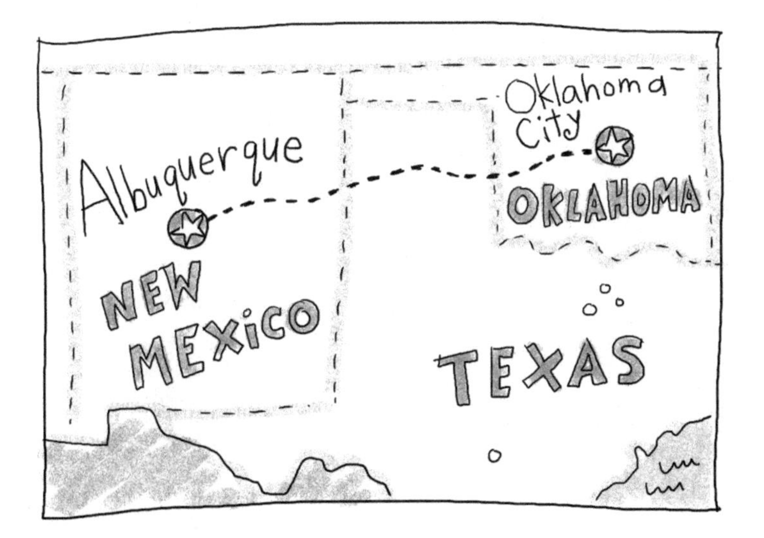

It's only 8:15 a.m., and we've already had one.

As soon as we got in the van, Dad said, "Good job getting up and out of the hotel so early. We have a long drive ahead of us. The trip from Oklahoma City to Albuquerque, New Mexico, is 500 miles."

When Dad said that, Kate got out her tablet. "Actually, it's 544 miles, or 875 kilometers."

"Thanks," he said like he appreciated that information. But I'm not so sure he did, because I saw him give mom an it's-a-little-early-for-facts-and-figures look.

Kate didn't seem to notice that look.

When she finished reading, she actually held her tablet up in the air like it was a trophy she'd just won. "What would you all have done if I hadn't come on this trip?" she asked.

I couldn't believe she'd actually asked that question.

Max shook his head like he refused to answer (which was a good thing because I know Kate wouldn't have liked his answer).

Dad didn't say anything either.

I think Mom thought someone should say something, so she said, "We're all glad to have you along."

But honestly, I don't think she meant what she was saying.

Mallory

AFTER LUNCH

Dear Trip Journal,

We just stopped for lunch and when we got back into the van, the problems started again, but this time they were a whole lot worse!

I was sitting by one window. I was sleepy, so I made a pillow out of my sweatshirt and leaned my head against it.

Max, who was sitting by the other window, got out his phone and started texting.

Kate was in the middle and she got out her tablet. I thought she was going to start reading something out loud and we were going to have a problem.

But Kate surprised me. She didn't read out loud. In fact, as Dad drove, she read to herself, and the three of us sat like that for a long time.

My eyes were just starting to close when the problems started.

"Who is Sam?" asked Kate.

My eyes flew open just in time to see Max snatch his phone away from Kate's sight and stuff it into his pocket. "Are you reading my texts?" asked Max.

Kate repeated her question.

"It's no big deal," said Max. "Sam is just a guy on my baseball team."

Kate wrinkled her nose like something smelled funny. "That's weird," said Kate.

"How's that weird?" asked Max.

"Because your last text said 'I think you're the best player on the girls' softball team.' Which makes me think Sam is a girl." Kate shrugged. "And yesterday you told her that you think her freckles are cute. Thats why I was surprised to find out that your girlfriend's name is Winnie."

I leaned forward. This sounded kind of weird to me too. Why would my brother be texting some girl named Sam to tell her that he likes her freckles?

I looked at Max. His face was turning as red as his T-shirt. Then he exploded!

"EVERYONE NEEDS TO MIND THEIR OWN BUSINESS!" he yelled.

Then he looked at Kate like she was the main person he thought should be doing that, and he started yelling things like (but not limited to):

"MAX!" mom said his name like he'd better stop yelling immediately.

Then she told max (who looked very angry) not to yell at Kate. She told Kate (who also looked angry) to respect max's privacy. Then she told Dad to pull over, and she made Kate and me switch places.

Max + Kate = a bad combo (like pickles with chocolate)

So now I'm in the middle of two angry people, which means a few things:

Thing #1: Even though I can't stop wondering about this girl Max has been texting, I don't think now is a good time to ask about her. So I'll just have to ask my questions in this Trip Journal instead of out loud. I mean, who is Sam? Why is Max so upset that Kate found out about her? And is Kate right that it's weird for Max to be texting her like this? Why would he be flirting with another girl behind Winnie's back?

Thing #2: As much as I would like to keep writing in here, I don't think it's a good idea. The people on either side of me could (and I know at least one would) read what I'd be writing.

Thing #3: Even though I've never been to Albuquerque and I have no idea what it's like, I can't wait to get there because anywhere will be better than being stuck in this car!

☹ *Mallory*

P.S. I'm not at the wish pond but I'm making a wish: I wish everyone will get along and be happy when we get to Albuquerque.

Welcome to
Albuquerque,
New Mexico
Yummy!

New Mexico!

WISHES DO COME TRUE

Dear Trip Journal,

Wishes do come true and not just when you make them at the wish pond.

When we got to Albuquerque, everyone's mood improved. We stopped for dinner at the Route 66 Diner. It was a really fun place. We sat in an old-fashioned booth and listened to songs on the jukebox. There was a hopscotch grid on the floor, and we all (even Mom and Dad!) played while we were waiting for our food.

We ordered cheeseburgers (my favorite, though it made me miss my cat and wonder how she was doing with Mrs. Black) and fries and milkshakes that were AH-MAZING!!!

We were having such a good time. Kate seemed to realize that the-who-max-was-texting thing was an off-limits topic. She didn't bring it up again. And no one seemed to mind when Kate took out her tablet while we were waiting for the check and read all about the history of Route 66.

Kate's Route 66 FUN FACTS:

#1: Route 66 is called the Mother Road and is almost 100 years old.

#2: Route 66 is 2,500 miles long and crosses through 8 states and 3 time zones.

#3: There's a famous song about Route 66. ♪ ♫ ♬ ♪

Even if Kate hadn't given us that last fun fact, I would have known about the song. It played on the jukebox three times while we were eating dinner. But it's a good song, so I didn't mind. We're at the hotel now and about to go to sleep. I just have one more thing to do before I shut my eyes. I'm making the same wish I made in the car.

I wish tomorrow when we see the sites of Albuquerque, everyone will keep getting along and that we will have just as much fun as we did tonight.

Traveling is a whole lot more fun when everyone gets along.

Mallory

A DAY ON THE TOWN

Dear Trip Journal,

Surprisingly, my second wish came true, just like my first one!

I'll tell you about everyone getting along, but first, I'll tell you what we did in Albuquerque, which is the coolest place ever.

It's nothing like Fern Falls. It's in the desert, so the plants and the scenery and even the buildings look totally

Where would you rather live?

FERN FALLS	Albuquerque, NM
Here?	Or here?

different from the ones at home. Plus, Albuquerque has lots of awesome stores, great food, and tons of fun stuff to do. I wouldn't even be upset if Mom and Dad said we were moving here.

Our day started at the Albuquerque Aquarium, which has over 200 kinds of fish. I can't remember all the kinds but I know we saw eels, seahorses, sea turtles, sharks, and jelly (no peanut butter) fish.

After we left the Aquarium, we went to Old Town Albuquerque. It's a village that was built a long time ago but that

has been improved over the years. So along with the original church in the city square and the other old, historic buildings, there are five museums, lots of restaurants, and over 100 shops!!!

We spent the day walking around and going into little stores. Mom and Dad let us each pick out one thing to buy. I bought some turquoise earrings. I also bought postcards for Mary Ann and Joey and Chloe Jennifer (which technically means I bought four things, not one).

When we finished walking around, Mom and Dad let Max, Kate, and me choose which of the five museums we wanted to go to.

We were going to draw straws, but Max really wanted to go to the Rattlesnake Museum, which has the largest collection of live (that's right, I said LIVE) rattlesnakes in the world!

Even though Kate and I were both kind of grossed out (and scared!), we agreed to go because Max really wanted to.

After the museum, we went to dinner at a Mexican restaurant and ate tacos with rice and beans. When our waiter told us we were eating New Mexican food, I told him I was glad because I wouldn't want to eat old Mexican food.

That made everyone, including the waiter and Max (who almost never thinks my jokes are funny), laugh.

It was a great day and not just because we saw sharks and rattlesnakes and bought earrings and ate new (vs. old) tacos. I liked it because everyone got along. Even Max and Kate. It was like she knew not to say things that would annoy him, and I think he appreciated it.

Max didn't even mind when Kate got out her tablet at dinner and read us some facts about Old Town Albuquerque.

I feel like we turned a corner (an expression I learned in third grade and which means when things change for the better).

We're all going to bed soon. Tomorrow we drive to the Grand Canyon, and I can't wait to get there!

Kate's OLD TOWN ALBUQUERQUE FUN FACTS:

#1: Old Town Albuquerque was founded in 1706.

#2: It was founded by a group of Spanish settlers.

#3: Most of the buildings in Old Town are made of adobe, which is the Spanish word for mud brick.

I'm just doing one last thing before we go to sleep.

Since I'm on a wishes-coming-true roll, I'm making a third one: I wish the rest of the trip will be as great as today was.

♡ *Mallory*

SHUT UP!

Petrified Forest,

346 square miles

National Park,

200 million years!

or

Painted Desert?

Van Troubles

IN THE VAN

Dear Trip Journal,

Whoever made up the expression "good things happen in threes" (which is something Grandma likes to say) did not know what they were talking about. Good things don't happen in threes, at least not on this trip.

My third wish did NOT come true. In fact, the opposite of it came true.

When we left Albuquerque, we had van troubles (and I'm not talking about the kind of troubles that have to do with the engine or the brakes).

I'm talking about the kind of troubles that happen when one person does something that annoys the other people they are with.

The problems started when we stopped at Arizona's Petrified Forest National Park. It's part of an area called the Painted Desert because the trees in the forest had literally turned to colored stone.

But when we got there and started walking around and looking at all of the

colorful rock formations, Kate got out her tablet and started reading.

She read about the history of the Painted Desert and how it started to form over 200 million years ago.

She read about the logs that fell into the mineral-rich swamp and became embedded with mineral crystals and didn't rot. Instead they literally petrified—turned to stone.

"Can you please put that away?" asked Max.

Max can be rude when he says things like that. (I should know, he's said plenty

of things like it to me.) But when he said that to Kate, I don't think he meant it in a rude way. Plus, I thought it was annoying that she was reading while we were all trying to look at things.

"Thank you, Kate," Dad said when she paused to take a breath. "That's very interesting. How about you put your tablet away for a while?"

"It's pretty cool here," I added. "Maybe you can actually look at things instead of just reading about them."

But Kate ignored all of us and kept reading.

She read about the size of the Painted Desert (which is 346 square miles).

She read about the dinosaurs that once roamed the Painted Desert.

Then she read about the erosion of the desert and how wind and water and soil changes continue to change the landscape of the desert.

Max and I rolled our eyes at each other like this was crazy. Even though Mom and Dad didn't do that, I could tell they were thinking the same thing.

Mom went over to Kate. "Why don't you finish up?" She even said she could hold Kate's tablet for her.

"OK," said Kate like she was almost done and would give mom her tablet as soon as she was. But then she started reading about the plant life of the Painted Desert, and she didn't show any signs of finishing, so Max said something (which I think everyone else was thinking but wouldn't have said).

When Max said that, ten things happened that led us to where we are now, which is back in the car, driving to the Grand Canyon, and NO ONE is speaking to each other.

THE 10 THINGS THAT LED US TO WHERE WE ARE NOW (WHICH IS IN A SILENT CAR!)

Thing #1: Kate started crying and said she was mad at Max.

Thing #2: Mom and Dad made Max apologize to Kate for telling her to shut up (which he's not allowed to say, but I don't blame him for saying).

Thing #3: I said, "Maybe Kate should apologize too, since she wouldn't listen when we asked her nicely to stop reading," which made Kate cry even harder.

Thing #4: Mom and Dad made me apologize to Kate for hurting her feelings.

Thing #5: Kate refused to accept Max's apology or mine.

Thing #6: Mom tried to explain to Kate why it is good to give people a little bit of information but not too much.

Thing #7: Kate said Mom was taking Max's and my side and that no one on this trip appreciated her or all the information she's tried to share and that no one wants her on this trip and that she wants to go home. NOW!

Thing #8: Mom said that was NOT true, that we were all glad she'd come on the trip. Then she looked at all of us like we should prove to Kate that what she said was true. So I nodded like it was, and so did Dad. Max nodded too, but I guess it wasn't very convincing because Kate started crying HARDER.

Thing #9: Dad said he'd had enough and made us all get back in the van (even though the Painted Desert is 346 square miles and we'd barely seen any of it).

Thing #10: We got back in the van, and no one has said a word since Dad drove off. (Except for Mom who said we are all acting like children, and I think by that, she meant very little ones.)

Grand Canyon, here we come.

Mallory

APOLOGIZE!
GRAND CANYON
This way
DRAM
The GRAND CANYON!
"We're here because we're here because we're here...."
We made it!!!
Sort of...
THIS WAY
GRAND CANYON

The Grand Canyon

ON OUR WAY

Dear Trip Journal,

We're on our way to the Grand Canyon, but no one is talking. We drove all this way and why? What good is a vacation if the people on it aren't even speaking to each other?

Technically, Mom and Dad are talking. But Max, Kate, and I aren't saying a word (at least not to each other).

Mom and Dad tried to get us to talk. As we drove away from the Painted Desert, Dad said, "Kate, I know it hurt your feelings when Max told you to shut up. That wasn't nice, but he apologized and so did Mallory. I think it would be

nice if you accepted their apology."

But that's not what Kate did. She reached into her backpack, got out a tissue, and blew her nose. Then she

dabbed at her eyes and made a bunch of sniffle noises like she was still upset and couldn't possibly accept an apology.

Honestly, it was a little too dramatic, and I wasn't the only one who thought so.

Dad made a *tssk* sound which I know was his way of saying he was just going to wait for things to work themselves out.

Mom put her head back on the seat and closed her eyes.

Max made an I-give-up grunt. Then he got out his phone and started texting.

I didn't know what to do, so I got out my journal and started writing about what was happening, which is what I'm doing now.

For the record, I, Mallory McDonald, am sitting in the backseat on my way to the Grand Canyon, writing in my journal about a backseat full of people who aren't speaking to each other, unless you count the comment Kate just made (and she made it under her breath like she didn't necessarily want it counted) about Max: "I wonder if he's texting Winnie or Sam."

Even though I'm mad at Kate, I'd be lying if I said I'm not kind of wondering the same thing.

??? Mallory

HERE AT LAST!

Dear Trip Journal,

We just got to the Grand Canyon and even though this last part of the drive wasn't the most fun part of the trip, I'm super excited to be here.

But it might be a while before we actually see the Grand Canyon. We just got into a very long line of cars that are also going into the park to do what we're doing.

Right when we got into the line, mom said, "We're here!" Then she actually started singing it.

Song: We're here, because we're here, because we're here, because we're here . . .

When she finished singing, Dad said, "Who is ready to have some fun?" Then he talked about all the things we're going to do here like riding mules into the Grand Canyon and going white-water rafting

I could tell both my parents were trying hard to change the mood in the car.

"I'm excited!" I said.

Max, who never says he's excited about family activities, said he was excited too.

Then, everyone looked at Kate. It was her turn to say she was excited, but she didn't.

"Kate, you love riding horse, so the mule ride should be really fun for you," said mom. She turned around when she said it and looked at Kate like she expected her to say something positive about how this would be fun for her since she does like riding horses.

"I guess," Kate mumbled. "But mules and horses aren't the same things."

Dad took a deep breath. "Kate, why don't you tell us some facts about the Grand Canyon. Now that we're here, it would be nice to know a little bit about what we're going to see."

"I don't think anyone thinks my facts are fun," said Kate like her feelings were still hurt from the last time she'd tried to give us some facts and was not about to give us any more.

Mom and Dad looked at each other and shook their heads like they'd tried and they didn't know what else to do.

Plus, they got busy doing other things. We just pulled into the hotel parking lot, and Dad is trying to find a parking space while Mom is looking for the folder with our reservation information in it.

"Our hotel looks cool!" I said as I looked out the window at a wooden building that was surrounded by trees.

I turned around to see if Max and Kate were looking too. Max was staring

out the window like he was taking everything in. But Kate was just sitting, looking down at her hands, like she didn't really care that we'd just arrived at a super cool place. She actually looked sad, and I felt bad for her.

"Everybody is going to have a great time here!" I said like it was a fact.

I hoped my cousin was thinking that "everybody" meant her too, but I couldn't tell what Kate was thinking. Even though not all of my wishes have come true on this trip, as Dad pulled into the parking space, I made another one.

I wish this will be a great vacation.

For everybody.

♥ *Mallory*

Disaster Strikes!

Yelling!

Shouting!

Lies!

Fight!

A Family Feud

DISASTER STRIKES!

Dear Trip Journal,

I can't believe what just happened!!! I expected a lot of things when we got to the Grand Canyon, but I never expected a family feud! Actually, what just happened was a whole lot bigger than a feud. It was a fight: Kate vs. Mallory vs. Max.

Here's what happened.

When we checked into the hotel, it was almost time for sunset. The lady at the front desk told us that sunset over the Canyon is beautiful, so Mom and Dad suggested we go.

"Awesome!" said Max.

But Kate said she didn't feel well and didn't want to go.

I wasn't sure what to do. I could tell Mom, Dad, and Max really wanted to go.

But I also knew we couldn't leave Kate alone at the hotel.

Even though Kate has been kind of annoying on this trip, I couldn't help feeling a little bit sorry for her. If I was on a trip with her family and I thought no one wanted me to be there, I'd be upset too.

"I could stay at the hotel with Kate," I said.

Kate looked at me like she was surprised I had offered to do that. I did a no-big-deal shrug. "We can go to the gift shop and look at souvenirs," I said.

At first, Mom and Dad didn't think it was a good idea to leave us behind. But we promised to be careful, and Mom gave me her phone in case anything went wrong. Honestly, I think my parents thought a little separation would be good for everyone.

So Mom, Dad, and Max left to go see the sunset and Kate and I went to the gift shop.

Kate seemed happy. I wasn't sure if it was because I had offered to stay at the hotel with her or because the gift shop had lots of cool stuff, but her mood had definitely improved.

Kate and I looked around for a long time, then I bought postcards for Mary

Ann, Joey, and Chloe Jennifer. Kate bought one too and said she was going to send it to her parents.

When we left the gift shop, Kate and I sat down at a table in the lobby to write our postcards. "I have to go to the bathroom," I said when I finished writing.

Kate said, "Go ahead. I'll take the post cards to the front desk and mail them."

I gave Kate the postcards I'd written to Mary Ann, Joey, and Chloe Jennifer, and then I went to the bathroom.

"All set!" said Kate when I came out.

So we went to the room. When Max got back to the room, it seemed like his mood had improved too. He'd taken lots of sunset pictures and was showing them to us.

"What did you guys do?" he asked.

I had a feeling Mom and Dad must have talked to him while they were out because I could tell he was trying to be nice. Which is why what happened next really surprised me, and NOT in a good way.

ME: Kate and I bought postcards. I sent mine to my friends and she sent hers to her parents.

KATE: (Looking like what she was about to say was no big deal, even though it turned out to be a HUGE deal) I didn't actually send the postcard to my parents.

ME: (Confused.) If you didn't send it to your parents, who did you send it to?

KATE: Winnie.

MAX: (Looking even more confused than I was.) You mean my girlfriend?

KATE: (Nodding) Yes.

MAX: I don't believe you. How would you even know her address?

KATE: Mallory gave it to me.

ME: (Not saying anything, but giving her a what-are-you-talking-about look.)

MAX: (Almost shouting.) Why would you give her Winnie's address?

ME: I didn't!

KATE: Yes you did. You gave me her address when you asked me to mail your postcards to Mary Ann and Joey.

You said Winnie is Mary Ann's stepsister and Joey's sister. And you told me that they all moved at the beginning of the summer, so I figured they must all have the same address (looking proud of herself for figuring that out, even though it didn't seem like something to be proud of).

MAX: (Looking at me, but pointing to Kate.) I can't believe you gave her the address!

ME: (Looking at Max.) I didn't give it to her. She took it! (Turning to Kate.) You said you would mail the postcards while I went to the bathroom. You didn't say anything about using the address!

KATE: I only took what was given to me! (Crossing her arms like she didn't think she should have to defend herself.)

MAX: But why would you send a postcard to Winnie?

KATE: (Not answering Max's question.) Why would you tell a girl who's not your girlfriend that you think her freckles are cute?

ME: (Not saying anything, but wondering the same thing.)

MAX: (Definitely shouting.) That's not any of your business!

KATE: Don't you think Winnie should know if you said that to another girl?

MAX: (Shouting even louder!) Is that what you said in the postcard?

KATE: Maybe it is!

When Kate said that, I thought Max was going to shout even more at her, but the person he started shouting at was me. He said it was my fault for giving Winnie's address to Kate.

That made me yell at Max that he shouldn't be getting mad at me. I reminded him that I was the one who defended him when Kate got mad at him for telling her to shut up.

Max yelled at me that that had nothing to do with anything.

I thought it did. I thought it had to do with me being a good sister and taking up for my brother. But he wasn't doing the same thing for me. "None of this would be happening if you hadn't been sending flirty texts to a girl who is NOT your girlfriend!" I said to Max.

"See," said Kate. "Even Mallory agrees with me."

But that wasn't completely true. Maybe I agreed with Kate about the texting thing, but she had said and done a lot of things that I didn't agree with, like taking the Winston's address without my permission. So I yelled at her that she shouldn't have done that.

Kate started yelling back (I think she was yelling at both Max and me) that this is the WORST trip she's ever been on.

Then everyone was yelling at the same time. I couldn't even keep track of what we were yelling.

Finally I stood up on a chair and said, "If you don't stop yelling, I'm going to get mom and Dad!"

When I said that, max and Kate both got quiet.

max plopped down on this bed said, "I've had it!" Then he put on his headphones and hasn't said a word to anyone since.

Kate plopped down on her bed (which is also my bed) and got out her tablet (and her headphones) and put them on too.

I wish I could say that I got out my headphones, but since I don't have headphones, I couldn't do that. I also couldn't plop down on my bed because somebody was already on it.

All I could do is sit at the desk in our room and write in my journal, which is what I've been doing.

No one in this room has said anything for a very long time. It's so quiet in here you could hear a pin drop.

Even if you dropped it into the Grand Canyon.

Mallory

START

The Bottom of the Grand Canyon!

SYRUP

Chowder

the BOTTO

Mule Madness

IN A BARN
IN THE BATHROOM
NOT COMING OUT

Dear Trip Journal,

After the fight Max, Kate, and I had last night, I didn't think this trip could get worse. But it did. It just got much worse!

When I got up this morning, I put on my hiking boots and packed my backpack with the stuff I needed for the mule ride into the Grand Canyon.

We all ate breakfast at the hotel. It was a quiet breakfast. It's not like Max, Kate, and I aren't talking to each other. We are. But mostly to say things that have to be said like, "Pass the syrup."

But a quiet breakfast was not my

problem! When we finished breakfast, we went to the barn.

First, we met our guide, Bob. He explained how we are going to ride the mules down to the bottom of the Grand Canyon, then spend the night at a lodge at the bottom, and ride back up tomorrow.

Then we met our mules, and that's when my problem started.

I could tell right away that my mule, Chowder, did NOT like me. He didn't look very friendly (not that any of the other mules did, but he looked even less friendly).

And when I was trying to put my things in the packs on Chowder's backs (the way Bob showed us how to do it), he kept pulling away like he didn't want my things on his back.

It didn't seem like Chowder wanted to take me into the Canyon. So I raised my hand and told Bob that maybe Chowder needed a day off and I needed another mule. But Bob said Chowder was fine.

When I got on Chowder, my problems got bigger.

He scooted back and forth so much that I thought I was going to be mule sick (the same thing as seasick, except it happens when you're on a mule, and not a boat).

I got off Chowder and told Bob I had to go to the bathroom, which is where I am now and where I'd like to stay.

But Mom just knocked on the door and said, "Time to go, Mallory. Everyone is waiting for you to start the ride."

To be honest, this is one ride I'm not looking forward to.

Mallory

AT THE LODGE

Dear Trip Journal,

We just got to the lodge at the bottom of the Grand Canyon. The ride down into the canyon was the scariest thing I've ever done!!! It was scarier than going to a haunted house on Halloween, taking a math test you haven't studied for, and trying to go to sleep when you hear noises outside your window, COMBINED!

As we started down the path, I was surprised (and not in a good way) at how narrow it was. I kept trying to get

This way

Chowder to ride as close to the cliff wall as possible. But Chowder kept walking close to the edge of the cliff (or at least closer than I wanted to walk).

I told Bob (who was on the mule in front of me) and he said Chowder was walking where he was supposed to be walking. But I didn't like it. Every time I looked down into the Grand Canyon, I pictured myself falling into it.

The further down we went, the more scared I got. "Bob, I hate to bother you," I said. "But I think I need to turn around."

Would have been better with guardrails!

"It takes some getting used to," said Bob. "You'll be fine."

But as Chowder stepped over rocks and kept going downhill, I was getting more scared by the minute.

"Chowder!" I kept saying his name and trying to get him to stay close to the wall, but it was like Chowder had a mind of his own and didn't care what I wanted him to do.

I was hoping Bob would turn around and say something guide-like like, "Sorry, Mallory. Chowder is one bad mule. Don't worry. I can take you back now."

Bob didn't say anything. He just kept going downhill.

But someone else said something, and that someone was Kate.

"Mallory, are you OK?" asked Kate. She was on her mule behind me. I could feel her mule pull up closer to Chowder.

"I'm scared," I said. My voice was shaking when I was talking.

Kate said, "I know riding can be scary when you're not used to it. But trust your mule. He knows what he's doing. Try to take some deep breaths."

I nodded and took a deep breath.

But right when I did, we got to a turn in the trail. (Kate told me later that this kind of turn is called a switchback.) When Chowder moved his body around the turn, I felt like I was about to go flying off his back into the canyon and I SCREAMED!

Bob tried to calm me down, but nothing he said helped.

"Mallory, relax," said Max. But I couldn't relax.

Then Kate said, "Mallory, it's normal to be scared when you do something like this for the first time. I was scared like this the first time I rode a horse. But it's going to be fine. I promise." Then she said she'd help me the whole way down the canyon. And she did.

Kate stayed right behind me the whole ride (which was over ten miles) and talked to me as we rode down into the canyon. I can't remember exactly what she said, but it helped me relax and not feel as scared about the height or the narrow trail or the dust clouds or the wobbly ride.

And as we got deeper into the canyon,

I actually started to enjoy the ride. I was even able to enjoy looking around at the rocks and plants and trees as we rode.

When we got to the bottom of the Grand Canyon, we crossed over a bridge and then we got to the lodge where we're spending the night tonight.

When we got off our mules, the first thing I did (after running to the bathroom because I really had to go!) was thank Kate.

"I couldn't have gotten through today without you," I said. And I meant it. Kate convinced me to trust Chowder, and it made me realize that I wasn't in any real danger.

"Yeah," said Max who had been riding behind Kate all day and had heard the whole thing. "You were amazing."

I knew Kate liked the mule ride down into the canyon, but I could tell she liked hearing what Max and I had to say even more.

♡ *Mallory*

STILL AT THE LODGE

Dear Trip Journal,

Something surprising happened tonight. Max and Kate and I were on our way to the lodge's restaurant for dinner. Mom and Dad had gone ahead of us to get a table. We were almost there when Kate said, "I didn't really send the postcard to Winnie."

Max and I looked at each other like we didn't know what to believe anymore.

"Then why did you say you sent it?" asked Max.

Kate kicked a rock as she walked. "I was mad that you told me to shut up. It hurt my feelings that you weren't interested in any of the information I was trying to give." She shrugged. "I wanted to get back at you."

"Wow!" said Max.

I wasn't sure if he was relieved the postcard hadn't gone to Winnie, or if he couldn't believe that Kate had made up that whole story just to make him mad.

She kicked the rock again and then looked at Max. "I'm sorry I said I sent the postcard to Winnie." Then she looked at me. "And I'm sorry I pretended I took her address from you." Kate paused. "The truth is that I actually did just write to my parents."

Max and I looked at each other, and I could tell neither of us knew what to say. So I just said, "Thanks for apologizing."

"Yeah," added Max. "And I'm glad you didn't really send a postcard to Winnie."

He looked like he was about to say something else, but just then a man in a big cowboy hat and boots walked up to us and said, "Right this way, ladies and gentlemen. Dinner is served!"

So we stopped talking and started eating!

♥☺♥ *Mallory*

The End of a Long Trip!
BLISTERS

A Wrap Session

BACK AT THE HOTEL
SOMETHING IMPORTANT
TO WRITE

Dear Trip Journal,

I have two important things to write.

Important Thing #1: Mules and I have something in common. The ride back up the canyon was a whole lot better than the trip down. Bob said the mules prefer it and so do I.

Important Thing #2: I'm glad Kate came on the trip with us. I'm not just saying that because she practically saved my life on the mule ride. Now that I've gotten to know her, I understand her a lot better.

Tonight when we got back to our room after dinner, Max, Kate, and I had

a wrap session. In case you don't know what that is, I'll tell you. It's when you sit around on the floor and wrap Band-Aids on the blisters you got from wearing boots on a mule ride.

It's also when you talk about everything that happened on the trip, which is what Max, Kate, and I just did (while we were bandaging our feet.)

The conversation started when Kate asked Max if he was still mad at her about the postcard thing.

"No," said Max. "But I don't get why you didn't just accept my apology. You didn't have to make such a big deal out of it. Pretending like you sent a postcard to Winnie telling her about Sam—that's kind of over the top."

"Well, it was a big deal to me," said Kate.

Max shook his head like that didn't make sense to him. "Mallory and I get annoyed at each other all the time, but we don't do anything that dramatic."

I watched as Kate adjusted a band aid on her big toe. It was easy to see she was stalling. "I told you I was just trying to be helpful and give everyone information," she said finally.

I could tell by the look on Max's face that he was trying to act like he understood. But I knew he didn't.

I did, though. I'd thought a lot about it on the mule ride back up the Canyon. And I'd realized that Kate's "fun facts" weren't really the issue.

"I think what Kate is trying to say is that sometimes it's hard to know how to act when you're in a new situation."

Kate and Max both looked at me so I kept going.

"I was really scared when I first got on Chowder. I didn't know what to do because I've never ridden a mule before." I smiled at Kate. "You know so much about horses and if you hadn't helped me, I never would have made it through that ride."

Kate smiled back. "I'm glad I could help."

I nodded and then kept talking. "Kate is an only child. So for her, getting along with other kids, especially on a trip like this where it's like we're all brothers and sisters—that's a new experience."

Max looked like he had no clue what I was talking about, but I could tell by the look on Kate's face that she was getting what I was saying.

I kept explaining. "Kate has always gone places with just her parents, and they probably like when she reads them a lot of information."

Kate nodded like what I was saying was true.

"Kate doesn't know how to be part of a bigger family because she's never done it. It's a lot like me not knowing how to ride on the back of a mule down a narrow canyon trail," I said. "Why should either of us be good at those things? We hadn't ever done them before."

"I get it," said Max. "I'm kind of in the same boat."

"Huh?" Kate looked at me to see if I knew what he was talking about, but I had no idea.

"With Sam, I mean," Max added. Then he explained. "Winnie has been my girlfriend for a long time. I just met Sam." He shrugged. "We're just friends. But I kind of like her. I guess I'm not really sure what to do."

Kate grinned. "Sometimes it's hard to know how to do new things."

"Yeah," said Max. "I guess it'll just take time for me to figure it out." He paused, then shrugged. "But that's why I got so upset when you brought it up. I felt like you were judging me for how I was trying to deal with it."

"Sorry if it seemed like I was judging you," said Kate. "I shouldn't have. What's that saying . . . you can't judge someone until you've walked in his shoes?"

"In this case, hiking boots," I said.

Max and Kate laughed at my joke, but then I got serious. I looked at Kate. "Even though we're cousins, I feel like I didn't really know you before this trip. But I'm so glad you came, and not just because I might have ended up at the bottom of the Grand Canyon if you hadn't. I'm glad we've had this chance to get to know each other better."

Kate grinned when I said that. "I'm glad I came too," she said. Then she leaned over and gave me a big hug.

When Kate finished hugging me, she looked at Max like it was his turn.

He held his hands up like there was no way he was doing the hugging thing, but then he told Kate he was glad she'd come too.

I could tell that meant as much to Kate as a hug.

And on that note, I'm going to bed. Tomorrow is a big day!

Mallory

Best Trip Ever!

6:00

FUN!

COLORADO RIVER

Going with the Flow

LAST DAY OF THE TRIP
BEST DAY OF THE TRIP

Dear Trip Journal,

I don't have long to write we just got up and it's only 6:00 a.m. (which sounds way too early to be doing anything when you're on vacation), but as soon as we get dressed and eat breakfast, we're going white-water rafting down the Colorado River. I think it's going to be a lot of fun.

G.2.G. (Got to go.) G.2.Y. (Got to yawn.) G.2.E.P. (Got to eat pancakes.)

Then we're off!

Mallory

BACK FROM RAFTING

Dear Trip Journal,

Today was AMAZING!!!

I don't even mind that I had to get up at 6:00 this morning. (I kind of minded when I got up, but not now.) I'm going to write out every detail of what we did so I'll always remember this day.

It started at a lodge that had a pool and a gift shop and a restaurant. When we got there, I said, "Hey Dad, maybe we should just stay and hang out here. This place is pretty cool."

Dad smiled and said, "This place is cool, but wait till you see where we're going."

I didn't have to wait for long because everyone who was going white-water rafting got into jeeps called Canyon Cruisers to ride down to the bottom of the Grand Canyon.

The ride down was tons of fun. If I ever come to the Grand Canyon again (which I hope I do) I'm taking a Canyon Cruiser into the Canyon and NOT a mule!

The driver (who knew even more than Kate) told us lots of interesting things about the Grand Canyon as we drove down into it.

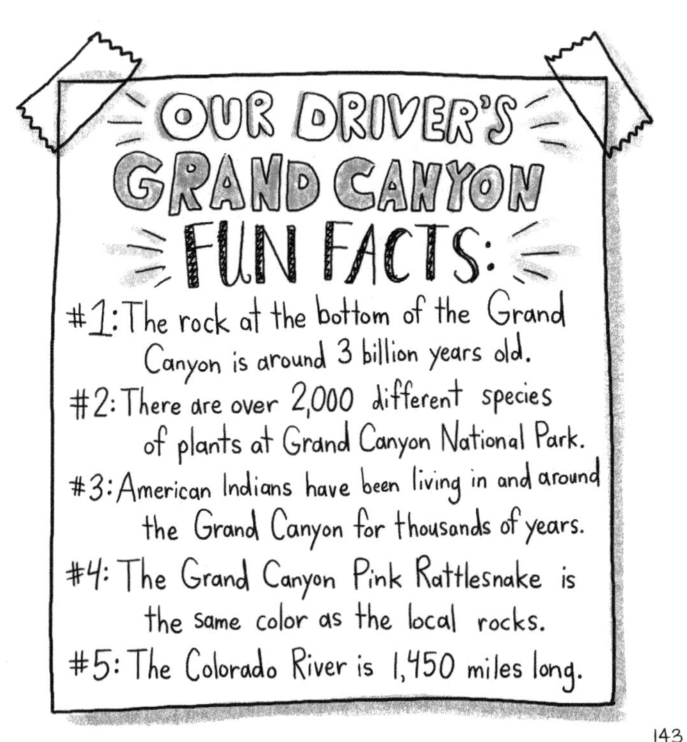

When we got to the bottom of the Grand Canyon, we met the river guides who would be taking us down the river. They confirmed that the Colorado River is 1,450 miles long.

"Don't worry," said our guide, Mike. "We will only be rafting down a small part of it today!" Then he gave us all lifejackets to put on and waterproof bags. "You should put anything in these that you want to keep dry," he said.

"Are we going to get wet?" I asked.

Mike laughed. "Soaking!" he said.

He wasn't kidding. We set out on the river in our pontoon boats, and as soon as we hit the first set of rapids, water from the Colorado River splashed into our boats.

I was prepared to get wet, but what I didn't know was that the water would be freezing. Even Kate was surprised.

Mike told us the water is very cold, even in the summer! But since it was so hot outside, the water actually felt good.

Going through the rapids was kind of scary at first. But once I got used to the way the boat felt as it moved forward over the rocks, it was more fun than scary. It was another case of getting used to something I'd never done before.

Mid-morning, we stopped rafting and went for a hike. Kate kept asking Mike where we were going, but all he would tell her is that she'd see.

Kate was really surprised—and the rest of us were too—when we came to a beautiful waterfall. It was the most amazing thing I've ever seen. (Even more amazing than when I saw Fashion Fran in person!)

We even got to go underneath the waterfall! A photographer was there, and he took a picture of Max and Kate and me standing right under it.

After we left the waterfall, we did more white-water rafting. Then we stopped for lunch and spent the rest of the afternoon lazily floating down the river and looking at rock formations.

There were several reasons I liked floating down the river.

Reason #1: There's nothing like it in Fern Falls. Even though I love where I live and all the things I do there, it was really fun to do something I can't do at home.

Reason #2: It was really cool think to think that I was so far away from home, but still with the people that I love most. I know that sounds kind of weird, but it was what I was feeling (and journals are for writing down what you're feeling).

Reason #3: When we were floating down the river, I could tell everyone was happy. Mom and Dad and Max and Kate and I were all smiling and talking and laughing.

We weren't just going with the flow of the river. We were all getting along and having a great time together. It made me wish that we'd gotten along this well during the rest of trip—but also really happy that we were having a great time together now.

You might think the day couldn't have gotten any better than that, but it did!

When it was time to go back up to the top of the Grand Canyon, we didn't take the jeeps up that we took down. We went back up by helicopter.

I, Mallory McDonald, flew in a helicopter!!!

Max was even more excited about it than I was. He said it was the high point of his life.

Even though the helicopter ride back was short, it was really cool. When we got out of the helicopter, Kate squeezed my hand and said, "I'll never forget this day."

That makes two of us.

Mallory ♥☺♥

OUR LAST DINNER

Dear Trip Journal,

I can't believe tonight was the last dinner of our trip.

We ate at a fancy restaurant in a hotel in Grand Canyon Village. Mom, Dad, Max, Kate, and I were all talking and laughing and enjoying the delicious food.

As I looked around the table, what I was thinking was that it was a perfect family moment, like the kind you see on TV ads but never in real life.

I guess I wasn't the only one who thought it was special. Mom did too. When we finished dessert, she asked a lady at the next table to take our picture.

When we sat back down, Kate looked at Mom and Dad and said, "Thanks for letting me come on the trip. It turned out to be the best trip I've ever been on."

I could tell she meant what she was saying (which meant a lot especially since she's been to some really incredible places), and I could tell Mom and Dad liked hearing it.

"Yeah, thanks," said Max. "It was an amazing trip." Then he looked at me like it was my turn to thank Mom and Dad. I would have thanked them even if he hadn't looked at me, but I didn't mind because he did it in a nice big-brotherly kind of way.

Now we're back in our room and Dad just said, "Lights out! I want to get an early start on our drive back."

I don't want to get an early start. I've had a great time at the Grand Canyon, and I'm not in a hurry to leave. But like Dad says, all good things must come to an end.

So for now, it's G.N.G.C. (Good Night Grand Canyon.)

Tomorrow, F.F.H.W.C. (Fern Falls here we come.)

Mallory

Memories

BACK HOME

Dear Trip Journal,

We're home again, and our trip to the Grand Canyon is over. The drive back felt like it took way less time than the trip there!

Kate just left to go back to Chicago, and I'm going to miss her. But the good news is that my family is going to Chicago over winter break to stay with Kate and her parents! And we all agreed that we're not going to waste one moment of that trip not getting along!

I haven't been to Chicago since I was five, so I don't remember much. Kate said there's so much to do and see, but not to worry because she'll be our personal tour guide.

Max told her she will make an excellent tour guide. Kate laughed like Max had made a funny joke, but I know he meant it.

I can't believe I'm thinking about that trip when I just got back from this one! Going to the Grand Canyon was so, so, so much fun!

I can't wait to make a scrapbook of all my great memories from the trip. I've already picked out some of my favorite photos.

I really like these before and after pictures that mom took of me with Chowder.

I also really like this picture of Kate and Max and me under the waterfall at the Grand Canyon.

But I think my favorite picture is this one of Kate and me. Dad took it when we stopped for gas and on the way home.

We'd been on the road for a long time so we were feeling kind of silly. But I like it because it reminds how much fun we all had together on our trip. Even though there were some bad moments mixed in with the good, it all worked out in the end.

I can't believe our vacation to the Grand Canyon is over. I also can't believe that the summer is almost over too and school is just around the corner

Fifth grade, here I come!

Mallory

Souvenirs

IN MY ROOM MAKING MEMORIES

In addition to all the great photos and memories I have from our trip to the Grand Canyon, I also have some great souvenirs!

I have a T-shirt.

And a snow globe.

And I have this little baby cactus that I brought back to keep on my nightstand beside my bed. The great news is that I'm not the only one with a baby cactus beside my bed. Max and Kate got them too. And I brought the same ones back for Mary Ann, Chloe Jennifer, and Joey.

My friends all love their little cacti, but I don't think they could possibly love theirs as much as I love mine. That's because every time I look at it, it reminds me how much I loved, loved, loved our trip to the Grand Canyon.

Darby Creek
A division of Lerner Publishing Group, Inc.
241 First Avenue North
Minneapolis, MN 55401 USA

For reading levels and more information, look up this title at www.lernerbooks.com.

Cover background images: © iStockphoto.com/drmakKoy (Route 66); © iStockphoto.com/leadlciceraro (cow crossing); © iStockphoto.com/duhal27 (café); © iStockphoto.com/professorphotoshop (boot).

Main body text set in Swister Regular 17.5/20. Typeface provided by Chank.

Library of Congress Cataloging-in-Publication Data

Names: Friedman, Laurie B., 1964- | Kalis, Jennifer, illustrator.
Title: On the road with Mallory / by Laurie Friedman ; illustrations by Jennifer Kalis.
Description: Minneapolis : Darby Creek, [2016] | Series: Mallory ; 25 | Summary: "Mallory's family is headed to the Grand Canyon. Mallory is looking forward to the road trip—until she finds out that her snobby cousin Kate will be coming along. Is it a recipe for disaster?"— Provided by publisher.
Identifiers: LCCN 2015024319| ISBN 9781467750295 (lb : alk. paper) | ISBN 9781467795678 (eb pdf)
Subjects: | CYAC: Family life—Fiction. | Cousins—Fiction. | Automobile travel—Fiction. | Grand Canyon (Ariz.)—Fiction. | Diaries—Fiction.
Classification: LCC PZ7.F89773 On 2016 | DDC [Fic]—dc23
LC record available at http://lccn.loc.gov/2015024319

Manufactured in the United States of America
2-42056-17187-10/10/2016